Let Peace Begin With Me

Volume 2

**By the Students in Third
through Sixth Grade at
W. A. Wright Elementary School
Mt. Juliet, TN**

WRITE TOGETHER™ PUBLISHING
Nashville, Tennessee

Published by Write Together™ Publishing LLC.
www.writetogether.com

ISBN 1-930142-71-4

Title: Let Peace Begin With Me, Volume 2. Multiple authors.
Subject: Literary Collections, Poetry.

Project Coordinator: Eloise Freeman

Cover Art: Jared Hollis, Grade 6

For Write Together Publishing:

Publisher: Paul Clere

Editors: John D. Bauman
                        Amy Rich

Cover & Book Design: Bill Perkins

To publish a book for your school or non-profit organization
that complements your academic goals or values, vision and
mission, please contact:

Write Together ™ Publishing
533 Inwood Dr.
Nashville, TN 37211

phone: 615-781-1518
fax:520-223-4850
www.writetogether.com

W.A. Wright Elementary

Veronica Bender
Principal

Jill Giles
Assistant Principal

8017 Market Place
Mt. Juliet, TN 37122
Phone: 754-6200

"Today's children are tomorrow's future"

KNIGHTS

Dear W.A. Wright Parents and Students,

   In celebration of our students' creative writing abilities and in pursuing our focus of making our students aware of the need for a peaceful environment, we proudly present to you, *Let Peace Begin With Me*.

   This publication was made possible by the generous donation from John Deal Company, JDC, and Sportswear Promotions.

   I would like to publicly thank the following W.A. Wright teachers: Ms. Freeman, Mrs. Keogh, Mrs. Lagadinos, and Ms. Fulmer. Your time and efforts are very evident in the quality of these volumes. I would like to thank the students for their individual writing pieces, and I would also like to commend the parent participation in some of the writing selections.

   It is the hope of the W.A. Wright Elementary Staff that all who read these volumes will enjoy and treasure them for years to come.

Sincerely,

Veronica R. Bender

Veronica Bender

Let Peace Begin With Me

Artwork by
Deshawn Jones, Age 8

My vision of peace is fairness, fair people and fair government. A fair government does not try to control the people. A fair person does not take advantage of that. Let fairness begin with me.

My vision of peace is cooperation. Cooperative government makes laws that are fair and sensible. A cooperative person obeys and abides by these laws. Let cooperation begin with me.

My vision of peace is fairness, cooperation, and many other things. I pray the prayer of peace over our country, and between the people and the government. Let peace begin with me.

Will Grenley, Age 12

One day I was playing football and someone wanted to fight. I thought for a minute, should I fight or not. So I asked, "Do you want to be friends?" He thought for a minute, and he said, "Yes."

Nick Oliver, Age 9

The butterflies and bees with flowers see. If the bees get pollen on the legs and go to another flower, it helps it grow. The same is true with butterflies. The wild is peaceful because it is quiet–fresh air and animal and waterfalls sounds. It is a good place to be. When the bears hibernate, they are real peaceful. When I am in the wild with my dad and brother, we feel relaxed. The wild is colorful and beautiful. If people use polite words and don't fight and stop killing animals and people, everything will be fine.

Taylor Hix, Age 9

In the beginning there was peace. But when Eve trusted a serpent and peace was lost, man cried out in war, and man dies in war. For what? Land, or to know who is powerful. In the end Satan will sit in the Temple of God, and he will declare he is God. Even though he is not, he shall say it. Christians will be in Heaven in peace, and peace will be in Heaven for all of time and longer. But until the time comes, we have to start with peace...one person...me.

Ryan Corning, Age 13

If I could make peace on earth begin with me, then I would in a heart beat. We all need peace every now and then just like we need love or water.

If I could make peace on earth begin with me, then I would try to be a better example to the younger ones. I would help people if they're having trouble at home, or if they're having trouble with anything. If a bully is being mean, then I'll just be nice to them even though that will probably just start a fight.

If we had peace on earth, everything would be different. There wouldn't be people killing other people; people wouldn't be getting raped; there wouldn't be fighting or anything like that.

That's why I want there to be peace on earth, and for it to begin with me.

Britany Pregal, Age 12

George W. Bush is peaceful. Al Gore is peaceful, and let peace begin with me. Let peace be in this world. Shooting isn't good in this world. Peace is good in this world. W.A. Wright has peace. My family has peace, and I hope this world has peace.

Zach Crooks, Age 9

How does peace begin with me? I can show others peace by getting along with people. Another good example is by helping others. I can also show other students the right way to act at school and church. It is also good to share with other people, especially those who are poor and don't have any money. These are just a few ways I can let peace begin with me.

Chris Chaffin, Age 9

If you take action, even though others may envy you, the whole world could live in peace. It could happen! Do your part, and soon a good deed will be recognized. All this could start with you! Let peace begin with you!

Nikki Bates, Age 11

Peace on earth is not something you can see; it's something you can hear and know that it's there. Peace on earth is the one thing we need to make our world a better place. You can't find peace just anywhere. You have to know it's there, and you have to tell people how peace is the best thing for our earth and environment.
Rachel Griffith, Age 10

You can have peace by picking up litter on the ground, even at home too, having kindness and friendship with everyone, and being loving and caring with everyone.
Kirstin Crockett, Age 8

Let peace begin with me and spread out into the world.
Let peace be for everyone and no violence for me.
Michele Smith, Age 8

If we had world peace, there would be no more wars.
There would be only love and smiling faces.
Anthony Sanderson, Age 9

I would walk away from violence.
I would ban all guns
To respect others.
If I saw someone hurt another,
I would stop them or tell.
Alex Hamann, Age 9

A sunflower is peaceful. Peace is when two or more people show peace toward each other. Love is peace. Peace is not when you argue and fight.
If you show me peace, I will show you peace.
A W.A.Wright student needs to be good all the time. My teacher, Mrs. Talley, is nice. But we still have to do our work.
Emily Ann Klunk, Age 9

I wish there was peace on earth. Everyone would get along. There would be no more fighting, no more war, no more enemies. Everyone would have lots of friends. I also wish we could stop using gas to power cars so we could have cleaner air so birds could fly safely. I also wish people would stop shooting rockets into space because if they don't, the world will be done. So if I started holding peace, maybe others would too. Then countless people would. If that happened, everything would be perfect. But, that isn't the story. If it were, the world would be peaceful. There would be no fighting, no shooting, and no one would get hurt so we would not need any hospitals. But if that was so, everyone could live in peace and that would be nice, but that isn't possible. So the world we know in the beginning would never be seen again.
Ray Birchett, Age 9

Let peace begin with me and I'll pass it on to you. You will pass it on to somebody else and they will pass it on and on and on until there is no one else to pass it on to. Then there will be peace in the whole wide world.
Alex Green, Age 8

The recipe for world peace is love, friendship, no weapons, no bad people, wrestling, no bullies, more teachers, doctors, and dentists.
Stevie Miller, Age 11

The world should have peace so we should have care, love, happiness, no bad, and we should have friendship.
Jeff Murphy, Age 10

I have a dream that everyone may have peace on earth and let it begin with me. Let them know who God is through me and the examples I set. I will not pick on people. I will not hurt or kill anyone. I will be kind to everyone. I have a dream that everyone would be nice to each other. I have a dream that all the schools will stay safe and peaceful. That is my dream.
Richie Rothe, Age 9

When I see peace, I see people getting along no matter what color they are. When I see peace, I see people helping people. When I see peace, I see no evil. When I see peace, I see me.
Brianna Smith, Age 8

I would bring Jesus into everyone's heart. If you have Jesus in your heart, you will have peace. Let peace begin with me. I would pray for world peace. Peace is for the world to share. Peace begins with me.
Ashley Crues, Age 8

If we take each day and treat others the way we want to be treated, there would be kindness and love in the world. I can follow the Golden Rule. Can you? Let peace begin with me.
Joshua Humphreys, Age 11

I would let peace begin with me by being a good example to other people. My mom always says to follow the Golden Rule. Do unto others as you would have them do unto you. If everyone treated each other the way they wanted to be treated, I don't think there would be any fighting or wars.

I would make it harder to get guns by making people have to take a drug test and making sure that the police knew who had the guns.
Ashley Fisher, Age 8

Friends always are there for you so cherish them always. Say, "Let peace begin with me."

Wars are going on. I ask myself, "Why are we fighting? God put us all here on Earth. Let peace begin with me."

What's the difference between us and people of color besides finger prints and skin? Let peace begin with me.
Torey Oster, Age 11

This subject affects me and my family closer to our hearts more than anything else in my opinion. That is because I have a grandmother, aunts, uncles and young cousins who live in a small country called Palestine, which is on the border of Israel.

This country is in a constant war between the people of Israel and Palestine over who gets what pieces of land and complete control over the holiest city of Jerusalem. This is not a war between religions like most people think, because there are Christians, Jews, and Muslims alike in both countries.

It is hard when I see the fighting going on with the adults the way they are. It is hard when I am talking to my grandmother on the phone and I can hear bombs and missiles being shot in the background, and hear and feel the fear she must have but never lets me be aware of. I get so scared that I can't help but cry out for help for my family.

When I see news reports of the fighting, I can see in the background the children of both countries playing and laughing. I have a dream, God, that the adults could learn so much from us children in this matter. Discrimination, my mom says, has many ugly faces. So I say, we need to teach these adults to make these faces beautiful again.

Peace not only begins with me, but begins with my generation, the next generation...Generation Peace.
Amanda Cason, Age 9

I wish that there would be peace on earth because everyone fights and some people don't get along. Some people are not nice and they are not good. The most people do is argue about stuff. I don't like people to argue because sometimes friends are not friends. Then adults argue and it is a mess up, so I want this world to be peaceful where everyone will get along. I want everyone to be nice and kind. I want there to be peace on earth so everybody will stop arguing and fighting. If there is peace, then everyone would be glad. I just want everyone to get along. So, God, please make this world a peaceful world. Please!
Katelyn Pewitt, Age 9

Please let peace begin with me because it would be fun to spread peace in the world. I like to play with my friends a lot. I have lots of fun playing with them. My friends are very nice to me. The thing I love most is going to church. Something I can do to keep peace is have lots of fun with my friends. And going to school would be peaceful for everyone. I could show everybody how lucky they are to have such a good teacher. And I could help my mom with the house. I would help my neighbor, Marshal. He works real hard sometimes. I like to help people a lot. I could help smaller kids with things like studying and homework. Or I could help my teacher with the room. My mom would like it if I cleaned the whole house. That would be a help I guess. It would be good if I helped my dad with mowing the lawn too. And I could help my friends with cleaning their room, or clean up all the dog messes too. Or maybe I could help my mother with the clothes because she hates doing the clothes. I mean really hates to! I like to help my friends the most though. But maybe I could clean up my grandma's yard. So please let there be peace and please let it start with me.
Kala Snyder, Age 9

I think the word peace means to love and respect people. Peace can also mean no war, not fighting, living in harmony, and getting along with others. I decided to write the word peace and make each letter have a meaning for peace.

P stands for Praying to God for His help
E stands for Equality
A stands for Awesome love
C stands for Change the world
E stands for Exchange views

Sunday morning I was watching TV. One man said, "To have peace is to stop hunger in the world."
Joseph Theiring, Age 12

I think we need world peace because Christ would love it if we could live peacefully together. It would make Him feel a lot better about mankind, and it sure would make this a lot nicer place to live.
Adam Sanderson, Age 12

What is peace and how can it begin with me? Peace is quiet and calmness. You have to have peace within yourself. You have to have self-control and self-confidence.

How can you have peace within your family? By being obedient and respectful to your parents. A family that goes to church usually has more love within the home. You need to be honest with each other.

What can I do to help to have peace within the school? It starts with no violence or drugs. You need to set a good example and have good behavior. Every student needs to come to school prepared to learn so they can have inner peace.

How can there be peace around the world? Country leaders should meet and discuss the problems. Countries need to settle their disagreements without having wars. All countries need to stop being selfish and learn to give and take.

Let everyone love everybody else. Let's all start by saying please and thank you. Let there be peace on earth, and let it begin with you and me.
Cody Partlow, Age 9

I am asking you to let there be peace on earth. Do you know what it means? If you do not, I will tell you. I will be at the march, so come by to see me. If you can, thank you. But I need more people. If you want to join me at the march, hurry like I do. If you come, I will tell you how I did it. I will be there at 1:00 pm until 3:00 pm. So come see me. I made some signs and they said, "I want peace on earth." I got four people to help me. Do you want to have signs? Yes! Make them and when you are done, come see me. Let's go. Thank you for trying.
Dalton Steele, Age 9

Let there be peace on earth and let it begin with me. Let everyone get along with each other. Don't let people make fun of other people because they look different or they talk different. Everyone needs to be friends with each other. If we get along with everyone, there would be peace on earth
Taylor Ralston, Age 9

My class and I are working peacefully today. We like that because nobody gets disturbed. While we are working, our teacher does not get disturbed by us. While she is working, she doesn't disturb us. While we are working in class, we get more work done so we get done quicker. We have less work to do when we have peace. We like it like that. So far, we have been good for today, and we hope we don't get in trouble any more so we can have a party in our class for good behavior. We hope we won't have to go to the office or have to get ISS. If we are good the whole year, our teacher won't have to get on us at all. We like not getting in trouble so we can be good the whole year. If we are good students the whole year and do not get one single demerit, we'll be the best students in our class. It is fun because we like having peace in our class so we have more time to do our work.
Michael Hogan, Age 8

Martin Luther King, Jr., was a wonderful man. He was always caring for others. Mr. King was fighting for blacks to get the privileges that whites got. Back when he was alive, during segregation, blacks could not do almost everything that white people could do. He tried so hard to stop that. Mr. King was always making speeches. Mr. King had a dream to make peace on the Earth.

Martin Luther King, Jr., got shot just for a speech about wanting peace on the earth. He was always trying to make peace on the earth, and he got shot for nothing.
Lindsay Dobso, Age 12

The peace sign is important because it shows that we mean no harm. The sign of peace is important during wars. This sign means a lot to many people. I hope one day that there will be peace on earth. I know that if there is going to be peace soon, it has to begin with you and me. So please spread the word of peace today. Tell your neighbors, tell your friends, tell everyone how important peace is.
Ariel Catherine Campbell, Age 9

I want to be peaceful. I do it by being a person of character. A person of character is nice, responsible, trustworthy, caring, fair, respectful, and, of course, has good citizenship. I am all of those. I'm definitely peaceful.
Miki McArthur, Age 9

Peace can begin with me by taking my brothers away (just kidding). I love both of my brothers, but there are other ways peace can begin with me like getting everybody to stop fighting. Peace really can get to me by God and Jesus. When I pray, I have peace because I think about God and Jesus. Peace comes to me when I'm at school and reading because reading really is peaceful because you have a lot of quietness. You can really have peace when you go into your room and lock your door and lay on your bed. But the best time you can have peace is when you're asleep. You can have peace when you're outside. Some of the time people don't bother you or yell in your ear or even hit you when you are just playing. When you had a bad day and come home, you can have peace if you go sit in someone's closet and shut the door.
Another way peace can begin with me is by making sure everyone is nice to everyone else. I will tell people to not fight, read a lot, go into a closet and shut the door, or go into your room, shut the door, and lay on your bed.
Another way is to take away guns so we can have a bunch of peace in our world, and no one will kill anyone. Another way I can have peace is if I am nice and my friends are nice back. Some more ways we can have peace in the world is for everyone to shares their toys and not leave anyone out of the games. We share peace so everyone feels good because some people don't have peace at home or at school on the playground like we do. They want some more peace too.
Kayla Costley, Age 8

The Ten Commandments say do not kill. We should love one another as Jesus does. Stop the fighting and shooting because that is not good. Lots of people die just because of one ugly person. That is why I try to be safe. I stay close to my family and together we pray. How do I want peace to begin? Make all the ugly people be nice and read the Ten Commandments.
Melanie Rice, Age 9

My parents teach us each day to treat people the way we want to be treated. They teach us to love everyone, no matter the color of their skin. I think that we should look at each other as if we were all brothers and sisters. With the help of God and the love of my parents, this is the way peace will begin with me.
Sydney Stegall, Age 8

I believe that peace should begin with prayer. When I come up to something hard, God believes in me. When he believes in me, I start believing in myself. I can hear Him in my heart saying, "You can do it, you can do it, Jessica, I know you can." He helps me in my prayers by telling me things in my heart or saving me in a car wreck. I believe that people should pray more about trees, animals, and poor people on the streets. People also should pray about our president, so we don't have to go to war. I would like to be a preacher when I grow up because I want to tell people more about God.
Jessica Ann Dozier, Age 9

One day when I was walking in the park, a boy pushed me in a mud puddle. I wanted to push him in the same puddle but I didn't. If people were nice to each other, we would have peace in the world.
Abby Burger, Age 10

To make "Peace Begins With Me Soup," put nice people in it and mean people. And then you put it in a pan. Put in water and turn it and get a spoon and stir. Then you will get peace.
Kayla LeMaster, Age 9

Peace is
  Quiet
  Friendly
  Nice
  Not mean
  Being good to each other
  Not saying bad words to each other
  Caring
  Fair
That's what peace is.
Cody Dyer, Age 9

To make peace,
    be friendly
    don't be violent
    help each other
    be nice
    be respectful
    be polite
    don't interrupt
    be quiet and peaceful
Chelsea King, Age 10

For peace to begin with me, I must do my best to be peaceful with all others. I need to forgive others when they do wrong to me. I need to forgive myself when I do wrong to other people. I need to learn and also teach that fighting is not the answer to solve problems. I need to do the best I can to show love and respect to everyone. When I do my best to do all of these things, then peace can begin with me!
Graden Gaines, Age 10

It's real peace.
It's real harmony.
It's real accord, agreement, amity.
It's real armistice, calm, conciliation, concord.
It's real hush, order, pacifism, quiescence, quiet.
It's real repose, serenity, silence, stillness, tranquility.
It's real agreeableness, alliance, understanding.
It's real compatibility, unison, adaption, suitableness.
It's real peace!
Samantha A. Murray, Age 11

I grew up on the streets of Baltimore. My dad had just passed away, and my mom was on drugs. One day I walked home. On the way, some kids asked if I wanted to smoke. I said, "No." That was one of the biggest choices in my life. That's how peace began with me.
Matt Hinson, Age 11

13

Why can't it just be: hush, serenity, stillness, calmness, no wars happening, peaceful, friendly, gentle, tranquil. Why can't the world have peace? And why can't it begin with me?
Caroline Sugg, Age 10

People know they should stop fighting and people know a person is special. It doesn't matter if a person wears different clothes or does different things or talks different.
Amanda Giorgianni, Age 8

To my family with love!
Peace is wonderful.
Peace is quiet.
I wish the world were at peace today.
When I think of peace,
I think of joy, happiness, and wonderful things.
Peace can touch our hearts.
I think peace will change the world.
Someday I want peace in the world.
The peace in my heart overflows.
Maybe someday everyone will have peace in their heart.
If only you could understand, peace is your friend!
Ellen Hinkle, Age 8

W.A. Wright Elementary School

Recipes for Peace

Artwork by
Randall Wallace, Age 11

1 1/2 cups respect
2 cups love
1 cup trust
2 tsp. caring
1 Tbsp. kindness
Dash of self-esteem

Directions: Mix all together and allow to emit from one person to another. Remember peace begins with you. Yield: A happy planet.
Genifer Langston, Age 10

99 lbs. hugs
96 lbs. kisses
107 lbs. love
6 lbs. compassion
106 lbs. non-violence
136 lbs. non-abortion

Directions: Always give hugs and kisses to show your love and compassion. Never, ever use violence, and be aware of abortion. Bake for 20 minutes and have enough for the whole world.
Paige Cutright, Age 11

4 cups trust
8 cups caring
2 cups calmness
3 cups patience
3 cups forgiving
3 cups giving
1 cup will
2 cups honesty
2 tsp. love
2 tsp. like

Directions: Mix & Enjoy!
Chris Brown, Age 12

3 cups peace
5 qts. happiness
4 spoons of love
6 gal. courage
8 pints helpfulness
3 cups kindness
10 pints amusement
12 spoons luckiness
11 qts. caring
7 gal. thoughtfulness
2 pints loyalty
8 cups consideration

Directions: First, turn on the oven to 350° and bake for 45 minutes. When you take it out, all of the hatred and meanness should be gone. Serves: 18 people.
Tiffany Paige, Age 12

3 cups smooth powdered caring
2 1/2 Tbsp. ground devotion
1 pinch of fairness
1 potful of respect
9 bowls of love
a little bit of acceptance
Ben Greaves , Age 11

1 whole part "Help others clean up their acts"
1/2 tsp. "Don't start fights"
2 Tbsp. "Persuade others not to fight"
1/3 pint "Help the elderly"
3 cups "Treat others as you would want to be treated"
1 jar "Respect everybody's opinion"
1 qt. "Don't be a bully"
3 tsp. "Don't butt in other people's business"
4 pints "Don't drink and drive"
2 gal. "Don't use drugs"

Directions: Stir together and you will get the best recipe for peace ever!
Nikki Bates , Age 11

5 cups trust
7 cups caring
1/4 cup following directions
1 huge cup character
2 cups respect
3 cups best behavior
1 Earth
All the people in the world
0 cups rudeness
0 cups meanness
As many cups of peace as you can get
9 cups kindness
10 cups Golden Rule
1,000,000 cups staying drug-free
100 cups alcohol-free
1,000,000 cups learning new things
10 cups compromising

Directions: Mix all together. Yields a beautiful world that begins with you and me.
Nikki Bates, Age 11

1 cup friendship
2 cups peace
3 cups love
4 cups truth
5 cups care
6 cups tenderness
7 cups respect
8 cups hope
9 cups faith
10 cups forgiveness

Directions: Take all ingredients and mix well. Then spread the recipe all over the world.
Ashley Hall, Age 11

I cup love
1/2 cup caring
1/2 cup sharing
2 cups non violence

Directions: Mix it all up and you have world peace.
Matt Collins, Age 10

1 tsp. no violence
1 large heaping of kindness
999,999,999 cups love
5 servings of violence (free teamwork toppings)
50,000 slices of peace
tons of hugs and kisses

Directions: Mix all ingredients into large bowl until smooth.
Pour hate-free water into large cups, half filled with happiness.
Add mixture to cups and bake for 30 minutes. Best served with
large glass of laughter and shared with many friends.
Trey Woodard, Age 9

1 cup love
2 cups harmony
7 cups humor
1 Tbsp. respect
1 cup good behavior
13 cups togetherness
2 cups affection
3 cups good citizenship
100 billion cups respectfulness

Directions: Take a giant bowl and put in cup of love and 2
cups of harmony. Then put in 7 cups of humor. Now stir with a
wooden spoon. While mixing, add a tablespoon of good
behavior.   When those ingredients are mixed, add cup of
respect. Add 13 cups of togetherness and 2 cups of affection.
Then add 3 cups of good citizenship and 100 billion cups of
respectful people. Stir all those ingredients and pour in cake
pan. Pre-heat the oven for 475°. Put the cake in the oven and
wait for 2 hours and 30 minutes. When the cake is done, wait
15 minutes for the cake to cool down. When cooled, frost cake
with Fun Family Frosting.
Katie Beach, Age 11

5 cups kindness
3 cups courage
1 tsp. friends
2 cups self-control
1/2 cup forgiveness

Directions: Mix kindness and self-control in a pan of bullies.
Let it sit for 1 day. You should end up with a world of kind peo-
ple. Then mix courage, friends, and forgiveness. Pour it on top
of kind people and mix it together. You should come out with
Yield: A world of peace.
Anna Cantrell, Age 11

1/2 cup	Working together
1 2/3 cups	Offer to help
1 1/2 cups	Respect
2 1/2 cups	Love
1/4 cup	Don't fight
1 2/4 cups	Peace
1 1/4 cups	Environment
2 2/3 cups	Acting nice
l/2 cup	Caring
l 2/4 cups	Express gratitude

Directions:
Mix respect, love, peace, and caring. Pour into baking pan.
Bake at 350° for 40 minutes. Pour in people working together
and people offering to help. Spread on expressing gratitude
and environment. Sprinkle on no fighting and acting nice. Let
set for 10 minutes. Enjoy your world peace cake and share it
with the world.
Brittney Moser, Age 11

2 tsp. love
1 cup harmony
1 cup happiness
2 cups giving

Yield: Peace.
Cory Cooper, Age 10

1 1/2 cups peace
3 cups love
14 cups less crime
5 cups less purse stealing
Chestieta Reynolds, Age 10

1 cup cheer
2 cups peace
3 cups niceness
4 lbs. no drug users
5 new homes for homeless people
6 lbs. of no violence
10 lbs. of happiness

Yield: The perfect cake.
Alex Lounsbury, Age 10

0 cups conflict
20 tsp. fairness
5 lbs. love
7 Tbsp. friends
9 lbs. freedom
50 tsp. niceness

Directions: Mix all the ingredients to yield Peace Cake.
Tiffany Pregel, Age 10

1 lb. love
2 lb. nonviolence
3 lbs. hugs
4 lbs. kisses
5 lbs. no drugs
6 lbs. flowers
7 lbs. goodness
8 lbs. niceness
Peace in the world

Directions: Just put ingredients in and stir.
Justin Smith, Age 11

3 cups trustworthiness
4 tsp. compassion
7 cups love
5 tsp. caring

Directions: Take the dough out of the bowl. Smooth it out the size of the world!
Callie Rice, Age 9

2 cups love
1 cup peace
2 Tbsp. good people

Directions: Pre-heat oven to 350°. Stir until ingredients are well blended. Put into non-stick pan. Bake for 10 minutes. Yield: 12 Peace Cookies to share with friends.
Christa LeRoy, Age 9

1 cup love
2 tsp. sharing
3 Tbsp. kindness
4 cups cherishment
5 tsp. friendship
6 Tbsp. sweetness
7 cups freedom
8 tsp. friendship
9 Tbsp. freedom from war

Directions: Mix all the ingredients together to yield peace.
Justin Tidwell, Age 12

12 Countries of love
7 Continents of happiness
51 States of caring
100 Cities of kindness

Directions: Mix all the ingredients together to yield a world of peace.
Ashleigh Akins, Age 10

1 cup love
1 cup peace
1/2 Tbsp. sugar
2 cups kindness
1 1/2 cups friendship

Directions: Bake in oven for 15 minutes at 340°. Let set in safe place forever.
Courtney Smith, Age 12

2 cups no violence
1 1/2 cups no drugs
1 cup world peace
1 1/2 cups love
1 1/4 cups safety

Directions: Combine all ingredients in a jar. Cover tightly and shake vigorously.
Ramon Guajardo, Age 8

1 cup love
1 cup equality
1 cup fairness
1 cup understanding

Directions: Mix together. Sprinkle with a cup of kindness.
Zach Budesa, Age 8

3 lbs. love
2 pts. respect
3 tsp. truthfulness
1 cup happiness

Directions: Stir up the sweetness until it has no badness to it. Pour it into a pan full of joy. Spread all of the thoughtfulness around so it fills the pan. Make sure you make enough to pass on to others. Bake it at 200° to cook it well. Let it set for about 20 minutes to cool, then pass on the Peace Pie to others.
Tiffany Stroupe, Age 12

4 cups compassion
3 oz. happiness
1 cup love
10 pints helpfulness
6 spoons forgiveness
2 cups peace
8 cups loyalty
2 pints caring
5 qts. hope
10 gal. faith
1 gal. laughter

Directions: Preheat oven to 350⁰. Mix all the ingredients together to make a heart. Then bake for one hour until done. When you take it out, all your meanness and hatred should be gone. Serves: 15 people.
Samantha Pearson, Age 11

3 cups peace
1 3/4 cups love
2 cups caring
2 1/2 cups respect
2 1/2 cups caring people

Yields: Peace.
Lisa Harrison, Age 12

6 lbs. hugs
6 lbs. playing
6 lbs. kisses
6 lbs. caring
6 lbs. smiles
6 lbs. faith
6 lbs. laughing
6 lbs. friendship
6 lbs. loving
6 lbs. family

Directions: Mix all 60 pounds of ingredients to get 60 pounds of me.
Taylor Schreiner, Age 8

Anagrams About Peace

Artwork by
Brittney Moser, Age 10

Let peace begin with me.
Expand peace all over the world.
Together we can bring peace to the world.

People everywhere can bring peace to the world.
Everyone should pitch in to help bring peace.
Anyone can help bring peace to the world.
Concern about peace.
Everything you do to help bring peace counts.

Begin peace with me.
Each idea of yours counts in peace.
Get moving and try to bring peace.
Include everybody to bring peace to the world.
No one should be left out when bringing peace to the world.

What can you do to help bring peace to the world?
Increase the peace in the world.
Too many times peace is not found.
Help bring peace to the world.

Maximum peace would be good for the world.
Exterminate the violence! Bring on the peace!
Tyler Mason, Age 9

Peace is great
Everyone has peace
A ball to get it
Cool is it
Even I have it!
Jenna Price, Age 8

People should love everyone.
Every day you should be thankful for what you've got.
Anything but violence.
Carry on the dream.
Everlasting love.
Paige Peterson, Age 8

Peace is cool!
Eat healthy food.
At home with family and friends.
Cats are special.
Enjoy sharing with others.
Brittany Syler, Age 8

Life
Outgoing
Values
Eager

Care
Active
Real
Ideas
Nice
Generous

Partners
Equally
Athletic
Care
Energy
Eric Baxter, Age 9

Lovely
Old world
Very peaceful earth
Earth

People
Earth
Animal
Citizen
Environment
Shannon Carter, Age 8

People
Earth
Animals
Citizen
Environment
Josh Cashman, Age 9

People
Earth
Animals
Ctizens
Evironments
Jessica Drennon, Age 9

Peace on earth
Earth is a good place
A good thing to do is not to fight
Celebrate peace
Everyone can make a difference
Britt Gammon, Age 10

People
Earth
Animals
Citizen
Environment
Danielle Duncan, Age 9

People
Earth
At work
Caring
Environment
John Langston, Age 9

Friendship
Religion
Individual
Earth
Nice
Delight
Ryan Peplinski, Age 8

People
Everybody
Agriculture
Care
Earth
Dustin Schotsch, Age 9

People
Earth
Animals
Citizen
Environment
Amber Lagunas, Age 8

People get along.
Everyone is nice.
Appreciate things in your life.
Care for one another.
Everyone be loving.

Friendship with people.
Offer a helping hand.
Remember to be good.

Must be kind to others.
Everyone is your friend.
Hannah Paulson, Age 9

Peace
Enjoy
Agreeable
Calm
Elated
Keashawn Hunter, Age 9

People live in peace
Everyone should live in peace
All people should not fight
Could you live in a world where all people fought?
Even we should love each other
Amber Moser, Age 10

Peace and joy is good for the world.
Easier to love than hate.
Arguing is wrong, loving is right.
Celebrating someone's birthday or holiday is sweet.
Eat healthy and be strong.
Jeremy Mosely, Age 9

Peace on Earth is good
Everyone who has lost someone to violence is mournful
An end must be put to violence
Cease giving weapons to minors
End was in other parts of the world
Caleb Hill, Age 12

Peace and harmony.
Earth could be a peaceful place.
Awesome people in this world.
Cleanest world we've had.
Excellent people are on the Earth.
Kayla Clarke, Age 9

Like people for who they are.
Encourage other people.
Try hard to like everyone.

Put others before yourself.
Educate yourself well.
Appreciate what others do for you.
Care for people and animals.
Effort brings success!

Be polite to others.
Enjoy being nice.
Go tell others about Jesus!
Invite Jesus into your heart.
Never be mean to people.

Welcome new friends.
Ignore the bad things.
Thank people always.
Help people in need.

Make friends with everyone.
Exercise your mind by reading.
Jessi Davy, Age 9

Why use violence?
Our pleas can help.
Rid this world of evil!
Let there be one nation - the world nation!
Don't choose violence.

Please help the world help itself.
Eck! War stinks.
A man's life shall not be taken by war!
Cool kids don't use violence.
End this senseless fighting at once!
Kevin Kemp, Age 10

Love one another
Encourage others; don't discourage them.
Talk it over peacefully; don't fight about it.

People should live together in harmony with one another.
Everybody in the world should do their part.
All lives are important.
Care about one another.
Everyone should be caring.

Be responsible for your actions.
Everyone should respect one another.
Give peace a chance to work.
I don't do drugs.
No one should be mean to anyone else.

We should make our neighborhood better too.
It is important to get along with everyone else.
Together we can do it.
Help each other to do things we can't.

Mind your own business.
Everyone should be nice to one another.
Stephanie Burnette, Age 9

War ending
Opportunity for a fresh start
Racism should stop
Love for everyone
Done with the fighting

Party for peace
Equality for mankind
All people join together
Create a world for everyone
Everyone love each other
Monica Manshadi, Age 11

Peaceful
Enjoy
Agreeable
Courteous
Elated
Jared King, Age 9

Pleasant people
Elated
Adore
Careful
Enjoy
Corey Caires, Age 9

People living together.
Everyone do not fight.
Always be polite
Care about other people
End to all wars
Tyler Bonnett, Age 9

P - let there be Peace all over the world
E - Excellent it would be with peace all around the world.
A - Awesome is having peace and we should all believe that.
C - all should Care about having peace in this world.
E - all nations should Evaluate their peace process.
Rachele Eckwright, Age 10

Problems to solve
Everyone be nice
And be responsible
Cancel violence
Everyone everywhere
Brad Hartman, Age 9

People get along.
Earth is good with Peace.
After Peace there will be no more wars.
Create a chain of Peace.
Earth is bad without peace.
Samantha Hood, Age 10

Love one another.
Everyone needs to share.
Together we shall live.

The world should have no violence.
Help instead of fight.
Everyone should love.
Respect those in authority.
Enjoy the friends God gives you.

Be a peace maker.
Eliminate hard feelings between each other.

Peace is a good thing.
Encourage each other to pray.
All should care about each other.
Cast your cares upon the Lord.
Everyone shall have Peace.

Over all this I see nice people.
No one should fight.

Everyone is to show peace on earth.
All of us should show kindness.
Remember people in other countries.
Treat others the way you would want to be treated.
Help people at all times.
Katie Weathers, Age 9

Peaceful
Emotional
Acceptable
Caring
Eternal
Jessie Petersen, Age 11

Peaceful
Enjoy
Amazing
Cordial
Elated
Tommy Hibbett, Age 9

Peace between people of the earth.
Everyone needs to try to make peace.
Anyone can make peace.
Come together to make peace.
Everyone would be happy with peace on the earth.
Jessica Morgan, Age 8

Pact
Earth
Agreement
Calm
Emotion
Anthony Parks, Age 11

Providence
Exciting
Acceptance
Caring
Excellent
Callie Gray, Age 11

Peace is good.
Exterminate all bad.
Assist those in need.
Care for others.
Educate all children.
Justin Garton, Age 8

Polite to people and animals.
Everybody don't do violence.
Always help people.
Care for people.
Everyone be nice.
Shelby Rawlins, Age 9

Patience
Equality
Acceptance
Caring
Eternal Love
Justin Collins, Age 11

Peace on earth is
Easy to find on a planet like earth.
And people helping one another is great.
Children playing on a playground nicely is
Easy to find on a planet like earth.

On this planet, there is peace on earth.
No, it's not that bad, because on this planet, peace is

Easy to find.
And the birds singing in the morning is peaceful.
Reading *Harry Potter* is peaceful.
Teachers teaching us.
How to find peace on earth.
Cody Feinstein, Age 10

People's
Effort
As
Citizens
Evolve
Randall Wallace, Age 12

Playful
Earth
Acceptance
Caring
Everywhere
Larry Donald, Age 12

Peacefulness
Eternity
Amiable
Calmness
Emotion
Vic Bogle, Age 12

People in America
Every day
And every night
Can live in peace
Everywhere and respect other people.
Kayla Long, Age 9

People
Everyone
Army
Community
Eternity
Miranda Edwards, Age 10

Peace is great for our earth.
Everyone needs to be friendly.
All of us should try to get along.
Caring is good and cool too.
Everyone needs to stop arguing.

One day everything could be better.
Nobody is perfect.

Everyone can make it better.
Anyone can help.
Remember that peace is what you need.
Trouble is not good.
Heaven is nice. Let's try to make earth like heaven.
Nikki Unland, Age 10

World peace for which we pray
Oh, yes, we should every day
Respect and compromise
Love and be wise
Do unto others

Please your mothers
Easy is not always the way
Anytime try to obey
Courteous is the way to be
Every day I'll start with me.
Meghann Hackett, Age 10

Peace begins with me.
Eternal love brings peace.
A war is not peace.
Capturing people is not peace.
Escape from hate is peace.
Brittany Patterson, Age 10

People
Earning
A
Corrected
Environment

Opinion
Non-violent

Everyone
Against
Right
To
Hurt
Taylor Wey, Age 12

Patience
Encouraging
Attitude
Caring
Equality
Brandi Gamache, Age 11

Please do not fight.
Everyone be nice to each other.
Always help each other.
Choose to give charity.
Everyone should always care.

Object to violence and unkindness.
Never stop caring for others.

Enlist people to be kind.
Apologize. Say I'm sorry.
Respect others.
Treat others the way you want to be treated.
Helping others is great.
Sara Morrisette, Age 10

Patience, love, kindness.
Everyone has equal rights.
Able to pray when you want to.
Courteous to everyone.
Everyone is their own self.
Shannon Gardner, Age 10

Working together.
Organizing peace talks.
Realizing our faults.
Loving one another.
Devoting time for others.

People trusting each other.
Exchanging ideas.
Agreeing on policies.
Caring for each other's needs.
Excellence in government.
Kristen Carver, Age 10

Please let there be peace
Each person come and join hands
Around our world
Come and make peace
Everyone before it's too late

On our earth is where we stand
New faces old faces

Either one we're all the same
As lucky as we are to have our world, let's make peace
Remember our earth is a privilege, so let's keep it safe
The world and our peace is important to you, and me
Hold hands to make peace with the whole world
Kayla Cottrell, Age 10

Determined
Remembered

Magnificent
All men to be equal
Reverend
Teriffic person
Intelligent
Non-violent

Loyal
Unhateful
Terrible he died
Helpful to all people of all races
Equal to everyone
Right for his doings

Kind
Intelligent the way he did his protest
Nice man
Great man

Justice
Remembered as a great man
Brad Hibner, Age 12

Working together
Okay to disagree
Resting from battle
Living together with joy
Dying soldiers get rarer and rarer

Peace around the world
Everyone is happy
Air is without gun smoke
Change of life
Every day is nice
Corey Wright, Age 10

Love your neighbor.
Enjoy your time on earth.
Together as one world.

Prepare yourself.
Everyone needs a friend.
Accomplish your goals.
Choose win-win situations.
Exclude bad thoughts from your mind.

Brainstorm together.
Expand your horizons.
Give instead of get.
If you fall, get back up and try again.
Never say never.

War we could do without.
Interact with your emotions.
Tell the truth.
Hide your hatred and anger.

Make every day count.
Encourage your friends to do good deeds.
Levon Emmons, Age 11

People getting along with each other.
Evict war.
A great settlement.
Concern for other continents or countries.
Ended war.
Daniel William Jones, Age 11

Peace on earth.
Everyone needs to get along.
Africans need to be treated better.
Cannot allow bad drugs.
Earth gives peace.
Amber Taylor, Age 11

Pleasing not to hear cannons and guns firing at night
Easier to cooperate with other countries
A peaceable place to live
Caring
Ending wars
Connor McChurch, Age 11

Pray
Enjoy life
Act happy
Comfort people
Encourage others

Open your heart
Never lose hope

Embrace the world
Avoid negative thoughts
Respect the Earth
Take each day at a time
Hold on to your dreams
Brian Dozier, Age 11

People shouldn't fight.
Each country shouldn't go to war.
A peaceful place should be our country.
Children can help as well as adults.
Each person makes a difference.
Caleb Knox, Age 11

Praying that others are happy
Everyone being successful in their own way
Achieving their goals without grief
Connecting with others in their time of need
Enjoy friendship

Making peace and harmony with others
Another problem solved
Kindness is what some people want and deserve
Enthusiasm toward new people
Situations that should be handled

Being the best you can be
Enraging towards others might not be a good choice
Trying to be nice and helpful
Telling others how to deal with bad situations
Entering the hearts of your fellow classmates
Rich not of money but love
Michelle Rivers, Age 10

Loving others
Earning awards
Teach peace

Pleasant life
Earning respect
Acting kind
Care for people
Ending violence

Becoming stronger
Everything will end up great
Giving to others
Is goodness
Nice and happy

Wishing good things upon others
Intending to say good words
Telling the way it could be
Helping those in need

Meaning no harm
Ending violence and putting in peace
Ryan Baxter, Age 12

War
Others
Religion
Love
Determination

People succeeded
Explosions
America
Co-operation
Equal
Sara Shelton, Age 11

Peace is the one that brought us together.
Each one should share their love.
A piece of love could change you and me
Count how many times you made peace.
Each one should go for their dreams not just sit around and
wait.

Begin with love and peace now, not later.
Each one should have the equal rights as others.
Gather everyone and tell them about peace.
In the time we die we will have peace.
Never give up faith.

Win the battle for peace.
In the time we don't have people.
The time we don't have peace
He the King made peace

My life should be full of peace.
Every one should have peace.
Anthonisha Lancaster, Age 11

Please let there be peace on earth.
Each person with kind hearts.
Another shooting in schools and another death.
Care for your peers.
Everyone love the world one day at a time.
Bailey Lester, Age 11

Peace is something we all need.
Even when you're mad, you should make peace.
At times you feel bad, make a friend and peace will begin.
Cry, pout, be stiff and stout, but don't let peace get out.
Every flower blossoms when peace is in the garden.
Mandi Sauls, Age 11

Pacifist
Equal
Anti-war
Caring
Enchanting
Whitnee Ferari, Age 12

People should love others.
Everyone show it.
American or African American, show some peace.
Color should not make a difference.
Even if you are black or white, show peace.
Charlie Brooks, Age 11

Pleasant
Endless
A very good thing
Can war be cured by peace?
Ecruteak is a peaceful flower
Drake Kossa, Age 10

Personal character
Earth
All people be kind and nice to each other
Caring for our brothers and sisters
Everyone get along
Paige Morgan, Age 10

W.A. Wright Elementary School

Very nice people are very peaceful
I will not be bad and hit people
O Lord bring us no violence
Let there be peace on earth
Everybody celebrate peace
No violence
Can everybody try not to do drugs
Everybody do not push or shove back
Misty Hite, Age 10

People
Everything
Awesome
Caring
Energetic

Interesting
Never

Me
Yourself

Helping
Oblige
Manage
Energy
Chance Holt, Age 10

People need people who
Encourage one another by
Allowing love and
Compassion to bridge all
Emotions
Beth Botts, Age 11

Life would be better with peace.
Everyone needs peace.
Together we can have peace.

Peace happens to everybody.
Everyone can have peace.
Almost everybody wants peace.
Celebrities need peace.
Even animals need peace.

Babies need peace.
Even people at war need peace.
Grownups need peace.
I need peace.
Never want war.

War stinks.
I like peace.
The people don't like wars.
Have we all had peace?

My dog likes peace.
Endure war.
Matt Smith, Age 12

Patience
Enjoy
Affectionate
Calm
Eager

Intelligent
Nice

Mature
You

Warmth
Observe
Reward
Loyal
Determined
Katlyn Snodgrass, Age 9

Let
Everyone
Try

Pacifist
Everything
Addiction
Central
Everywhere

Better
Establish
Generate
Invigorate
Noisy

Wisdom
In
Towards
Helping

Myself
Everyone
Gary Sircy, Age 11

Preparing for the big ugly war.
Escaping from everyone.
Armed with soldiers and big guns.
Carrying injured soldiers to safe spots.
End of war. Peace has begun
Chris Earles, Age 11

People care for others
Even if we are different
And everyone can help
Change our mean ways
Every chance we get.
Leah Kraemer, Age 8

Love is shown with the heart.
Everybody should be friendly.
Tobacco shouldn't be sold.

People shake hands to make peace.
Elephants are very peaceful.
A person sometimes can be mean.
Can you have peace in your heart?
Exactly what is peace?

Bringing gifts can make peace.
Every day I try to be friendly.
God, can You make peace on earth?
In most countries, there is not peace.
Never should we fight.

Weapons cannot make peace.
I keep peace in my house.
Too many people are violent.
Helping people make peace is fun.

May I bring peace among us.
Excellent people bring peace to all.
Zak Lind, Age 9

People
Everybody
Anybody
Children
Everywhere
Ashley Bishop, Age 12

Working together
On the earth
Right is not wrong
Loving others
Do your best
Brendan Neugent, Age 10

People need peace
Everyone likes it
Aren't you going to let peace begin with you?
Can we make peace?
Everyone thinks peace is cool.
Brooke Thacker, Age 8

Peace in Poems

Artwork by
Beth Botts, Age 10

Let there be peace on earth
And let the people see
That peace on earth
Is starting with me.
Shawn Snyder, Age 10

No more fighting, no no no
No more more crying, no no no
No more broken hearts of deaths
From those horrid wars, no no no
Just peace, yeah peace, nothing else
But peace all over the world
Just peace, yeah peace,
I don't want any more crying
Over deaths of loved ones, yeah peace,
No more bombing, no more guns
Just laughing, smiling faces, and peace
Just peace
Amanda Sutton, Age 10

Peace can happen everywhere
It can begin with me.
Peace occurs when people care
It occurs when people share.
Peace is free
It can start with me
Andrea Sherwood, Age 12

Shake the hands of your fellow friends and foes.
Whether black or white.
Be nice if you don't want a fight.
That's just what is right.
So shake the hands of your fellow friends and foes.
Kayla Brown, Age 11

I heard about a man
Named Dr. King,
He had a great speech
Called "I Have a Dream"
Yeah, he was really famous and all,
He preached the word and fought for new laws.

I try to be like him,
To give a helping hand
And be fair to my friends.
Peace with me: yeah, that's my game.
You've heard my dream and it's never gonna change.
Josh Giles, Age 8

Peace on earth, peace on earth
Let there be peace in every birth.

Let no more wars ever be fought
Let there be peace in every thought.

Let there be peace in every day
And let that peace always stay.

Let everyone be as peaceful as a bird
Let there be peace in every word.
Spenser Johnston, Age 10

People, People, Let love begin.
People, People, Let peace begin.
People, People, Can't you see?
People, People, Peace begins with you and me.
People, People, It's not hard.
People, People, Let's do our part.
People, People, Don't you know?
Peace and love will always flow.
Caitlin Smith, Age 12

Let Peace Begin with anything.
Let Peace Begin with kids.
Let Peace Begin with women.
Let Peace Begin with men.
Let Peace Begin with you.
Let Peace Begin with me.
Allison Goodwin, Age 11

Peace can start with you.
Peace can start with John or Sue.
Can I help?
Is there anything I can do?
Tell people what peace can do.
What a difference a small word can do.
Daryl Johnson, Age 12

Let Peace begin with us
You will see what will happen
If you let peace begin with us
Dustin Murphy, Age 12

The other day I thought,
What if no one ever fought?
This world would have peace
And all bad things would cease.
Things like envy, fighting, and hate
They would stop before it's too late.
And kids would always respect each other
By making each of us their brother.
Again, I thought, for peace to start
These things must change within *my* heart.
Kimberly Rollins, Age 9

Peace is something the world should have.
Peace is something the world should do.
If we use it wisely, the world would not be broken in two.
Antwaun Majors , Age 11

Let peace begin with me.
Let the whole world see
How nice peace can be.
So let peace start with you and me.
Alex Raymer, Age 10

Peace in this world is very low
We need to bring it up and make it show.
Although it is hard for some people to do,
Just follow me and you'll make it through.

All these wars and violence
Just don't even make any sense.
One little quarrel can become a big one
And then that leads to a gun.

Too many people fight today.
We just let it go and stay that way.
That can be changed, just you see,
All because it can start with me.
Paige Thomas, Age 11

Peace is sweet, so can't you see
That everyone needs Peace?
People don't see that you and me
Can make this world more happy.

If all we did was fight, fight, fight,
The world would be over overnight.
If you don't see that we need peace
Then open your eyes and look on the streets.

Peace can begin with you and me
So get up and do your part
To make this world have love in its heart.
Meagin Maddox, Age 12

Let peace begin with us.
Let peace begin with us.
Let peace begin with us.
Quit the stealing,
Quit the gangs,
Quit the violence,
Quit the guns,
If all this could come true,
The world would be a peaceable place
For me and you.
Nick Gibby, Age 11

I believe that everyone can do something
To make the world a better place
Even if it is just a little
Prayer of grace.

I believe in peace.

You can do something big to help,
or something small,
Even if it is a simple hug.

I believe in Peace.
Mandy Davis, Age 11

Peace in the world is a nice thing to have.
Peace in the world, let's join and laugh.
Peace in the world bring to our nation.
Let's have a celebration.
Peace in the world, no crime and no hate.
Peace in the world, let's all just relate.
Matt Majors, Age 12

No guns or violence in Providence
No wars at Vietnam
No fights with Cuba or Germany
Let's all get along
I heard about Columbine
Let it be all the time
Guns are bad in different ways
Let's carry on our lives throughout our days

Peaceman, Peaceman
Smiles in different lands
Peaceman, Peaceman
We all need a helping hand.

Open up your eyes
It would be a surprise
How many miles
It would be
So please
Get together
In the bright wonderful weather
So please let our dream
Come true
Thanks for trying
To stop the dying
To keep our world clean
From all the deaths we have seen

Peaceman, Peaceman
Smiles in different lands
Peaceman, Peaceman
We all need a helping hand
Peaceman, Peaceman
Asa Ellithorpe, Age 11
Cody Chandle, Age 11

There is peace in your future
There is peace in your home
There is peace in the present
There is peace on the phone

Peace can really change our lives
If you can see the change in me
That is where I want to be
Living in peace and harmony
Gregg Medlin, Age 10

Let Peace Begin With Me and every other child,
Let Peace Begin With Me, it will be worth your while,
Let Peace Begin With Me, spread it throughout the world,
Let Peace Begin With Me, I'll start with every boy and girl,
Let Peace Begin With Me
Let Peace Begin With Me
Cameron W. Nolan, Age 12

Let me be nice to my friends,
and they will be nice to me.
Let me be nice to my parents,
and they will be nice to me.
Let me be nice to all others,
and what a wonderful world it would be.
Jamie Vance, Age 9

Peace on earth is what we need.
So just let peace begin with me.
People should not kill.
But there is no stopping them,
Sure enough they will.

All people should try to make peace.
But for some, that is what they will do the least.
Everyone should try to quit drugs,
Because if they don't, they will have bugs.
Joe Thomas, Age 10

Let's all not sit around and wait for a job to be done,
When the hope for world peace could be won.
It takes me and you, now what will you do?
So everyone be like Martin Luther King,
And let the bells of world peace ring.
What will you do because it starts with me and you?

So if world peace was number one in everyone's heart,
None of the people would be divided apart.
Treat others as you want to be treated, that's the golden rule,
If everyone went by that, the world wouldn't be so cruel.
Remember it takes you and me, and me and you,
And now that's what we need to do.
Hannah Irwin, Age 11

Let there be peace
For all the world
And at the very least
Let peace begin with me

For all the people
Let there be peace and harmony
Let's all be friends
And have no enemies

Wouldn't it be great
If there was no hate?
So let's be friends before it's too late
Let peace begin with me
Shelby Kennedy, Age 11

Be kind.
Be neat.
Be sweet.
Don't smoke around me.

Don't be selfish.
Don't do drugs.
That's what peace is all about.
Amber Venable, Age 11

Love, love is like a stream
It keeps flowing
Love, love is something in all of us.
It never dies.
It keeps growing.
Love, love is like you and me.
It beats evil.
Garrett Frazier, Age 9

Peace on Earth for many men,
No bombs, no wars, we'd all be friends.
Blue skies, white clouds, pretty rainbows,
No guns, no knives, and no more sorrows.
I pray to God for all to see,
My very wish of peace I seek.
Hayden Hix, Age 9

One is for the love that I'm feeling in my heart.
Two is reaching out and helping love to start.
Three is for a message–a message that I care.
Four is for the courage to spread it everywhere.
Five's a helping hand for those who are in need.
Six is for the joy that comes with each good deed.
Seven is accepting that we've many points of view.
Eight is for the patience to work problems through.
Nine's a wish for freedom that would bring us all release.
Ten is for the dream of a world all joined in peace.
Troy McDonald, Age 9

I could clean the grass.
And for people to be nice, friendly.
For people not to kill and no drugs.
For people to be fun and no fighting.
Fun
Friendly
Nice
Funny
Steven Wills, Age 9

Let there be peace on earth.
Let us stop all the hate.
Let there be peace on earth
And love one another.
Let there be peace on earth
Let us stop the killings.
Let there be peace on earth
Let us follow the golden streets.
Let there be peace on earth
Let us go where there is no more pain.
Let there be peace on earth
Let us escape from this place.
Shelby Morgan, Age 8

Let peace begin with me
And then you will see
What peace on Earth can bring
If peace can begin with me.
Sydney Wilbourn, Age 11

Let peace begin with me.
Let peace end with me.
Lorne Thomas, Age 9

Peace to me is...
caring
sharing
being nice
stopping wars
Declaration of Independence
helping others
Lindsey Young, Age 9

Peace, Peace
What is peace?
Well, we know what it's not.
It's not violence
And it's not war.
Oh, so now I get it–
Peace is not about violence,
And it's not about war,
So it must be about freedom and helping others.
Oh yeah,
Peace is about freedom and helping others.
Avery Dobbs, Age 8

Peace
Freedom
Happiness
Love
make a
difference
in the world
always.
Mark Dyer, Age 9

Let Peace Begin with Me
With You
With Everything
And
With Everyone
Too!
Anthony Bennett, Age 9

Peace
Quiet, safe, great
Stops the war.
Kelsie Richards, Age 8

W.A. Wright Elementary School

Artwork by
Brian Dozier, Age 11

Let peace begin with me
And I will guarantee
That if you stick with me
I'll let peace begin with me
Wars are going on
Stores are being robbed
People are being killed
But if you stick with me
I'll let peace begin with me
Countries are being bombed
People are being hurt
Things are being stolen
But if you stick with me
I'll let peace begin with me
People are being kidnapped
Things are being burned
Rocks are thrown at houses
Cars are being egged
But if you stick with me
I'll let peace begin with me
So if you stick with me
I will guarantee
I'll let peace begin with me.
Krystal M. Smith, Age 10

Let peace begin with me.
Peace is wonderful,
Can't you see
Drugs and things like alcohol,
You shouldn't do that stuff at all.
Tobacco is bad,
And it really makes me mad
When you have to do a drug
But you don't have time to give a hug.

Pick the right choices.
Make the right decisions.
I hope you've learned a lesson.
Let peace begin with each of us.
Amber Bratcher, Age 11

Let there be peace
Shout it out with glee
Let there be peace
Let everyone be free
Peace should be for everyone
Not just you and me
But everyone in the world
From sea to shining sea
Let there be peace
There's nothing else to say
Let there be peace on earth
Every single day.
Kayla Patterson, Age 10

No more violence, shooting, and fighting.
No more bad words and hurtful writing.
This is the world I see in my mind.
All the people will be very kind.
Brothers and sisters sharing their toys.
Caring and loving with lots of joy.
Thumbs up, high fives and winks of love.
Spread kindness that comes from above.
Peace is kindness we all should do.
And peace is something you can do.
Jerica Kinnard, Age 9

Let peace on Earth
Begin with me because
I am the Earth and the
Earth is me. Each blade
Of grass, each honey tree,
Each bit of mud, and stick
And stone is blood and muscle,
Skin and bone.

And just as I
Need every bit of
Me to make my body
Fit, so Earth needs
Grass and stone and tree
And things that grow
Here naturally.
As long as life
Is dear and free,
Please let Peace
Begin with Me.
Latoya Crittenden, Age 9

Stop the violence,
Let there be silence.
No more guns,
They're not fun.
Let there be peace in the world,
For every boy and girl.
Blake Newberry, Age 9

Peace is being nice.
Peace is cool.
Peace is awesome.
Peace is coming together.
Peace is not fighting at all.
Peace is loving each other.
I live in peace.
Taylor Hall, Age 11

Let there be peace
Conflict be gone
Let there be peace
Violence is wrong

Let there be peace
All through the world
Let there be peace
The earth is a pearl

Let there be peace
Right here with you
Let there be peace
With me, too
Nick Jones, Age 11

Let peace begin with me.
And here is what I know.
If we will keep God first.
Peace is sure to grow.
Jesus is the only way.
Just read the words below.
Plainly said, plainly read...
No Jesus. No Peace.
Know Jesus, Know Peace.
Devin Drake, Age 9

I smile at everyone I see.
Let peace begin with me.
I lend a helping hand for free.
Let peace begin with me.
I let my friends be who they want to be.
Let peace begin with me.
God lives in me for eternity.
Let peace begin with me.
I believe in one nation under God and liberty.
Let peace begin with me.
I believe in God, you see.
So peace does begin with me.
Brooke Jefcoat, Age 9

Let there be peace in schools
And let it be cool
Let kids be nice to one another
While they talk to each other.
That's the saying my mother said.
Now let there be peace
And let it begin with me.
Logan Collins, Age 10

Peace is a sympathetic thing
It will not come in just one ring
It will not say I'll be there for you
Without going somewhere else through and through
So if you will take advice from me
Let peace out so everyone can see.
Brandi Griggs, Age 10

I pray each night for peace and love.
I would say a few words to the Lord above.
I hope we can have peace soon for everyone's sake.
You know we all make mistakes.
So let it be peace and not fight against one another.
Because in God's eyes we are all sisters and brothers.
So when you look into my face,
"Let it begin with me"
In God's grace.
Amanda Brown, Age 10

Stories About Peace

Artwork by
Trey Drinkard, Age 8

Once upon a time, there was a boy named Taylor. He liked to play with his friends. But one day he had a lot of homework. Then there was a sound. "Knock, Knock." There was someone at the door. He didn't want to go outside, and so he answered the door. It was Tyler. Taylor wanted to do his homework. "I can't play. I have to do homework." "Come to my house when you're done." "Okay." So he went back inside and was doing his homework. "Knock, Knock." Someone was at the door, so he answered the door. It was Bill. "Can you play?" "No, I have homework." BAM – he slammed the door. Can't a boy have any peace around here? So he started back to his homework. "Knock, Knock." "I'm not home," he said. "I need peace." He wanted peace, but he couldn't get it. He was almost done with his first lesson when someone knocked at the door. But it was just the mailman. So he got done with his first lesson and started on his second lesson. "Knock, Knock." He was about to pull his hair out! It was Bill again. "Give me peace." And so he went back inside and did his homework and there it was again. He didn't answer. He just did his second lesson. Then his mom wanted him to take out the trash. "I'm doing my homework." So he kept doing his homework so he could go outside. He got done with his second lesson, and then moved on his last lesson. "Ding Dong." The doorbell. It was the cable company arriving to fix the TV. It was so loud, he went to a different room and did his homework. He was almost done when "Knock, Knock." Someone was at the door, and it was Jack. "I can't play. I will be a few minutes." "Okay."

And then he was done with his homework, and he went outside to play.
Taylor Wilson, Age 9

Peace begins when a fight starts and I help. Like when three friends were in a fight and they could not stop fighting, until I came along and helped them solve their problem. We four became friends for life.

There was another time when two other friends and I were in a fight, and it went on for a while where nobody talked to anyone. There were times when we cried and times when we could not think. Then that's when I said, "This is stupid. We should just be friends and stop this fighting." And then we became lifetime friends.
Daleigh Henderson, Age 12

Once upon a time long ago, there lived a girl named Heather. In her country, the people had a war over who was better. The men threw car bombs and women threw pots and dishes. Ladies threw rattles and dirty diapers. It was horrible. One day at Heather's school, the kids and teachers started to fight, except for Heather. She knew what she had to do. Later that day, when she was playing on the swings, she knew she just had to fight for world peace. She jumped out of the swing so fast she did a summersault and almost broke her neck. She ran and ran for thirty minutes non-stop. Finally when she reached the gates, she yelled, "Stop." All the people looked at her. Heather said, "Why are we fighting. Who's hurt?" "Ugh, ugh, ugh," they shouted.

Later that night, the people could not sleep. They were ashamed of themselves and how they had treated the little girl. As the sun rose, Heather's eyes opened with happiness because the people did not start a war from then on. Instead they worked together and built a town called "Heathertown." It was a free town. Of course Heather grew up and went all around the world to try to get people to fight for world peace and justice and, most important, for America.

Amber Marie Mitchell, Age 8

Artwork by Brett Schultz, Age 11

Far, far away, there is a door of peace. Nobody knows what is behind that door. At school, some bad boy says it's just a phony folk tale. When I got off the bus at my grandpa's house, I asked him if that door of peace thing was true. He said it is if you think it is. My grandpa said that he learned it from his dad and he said it is in your heart. He said that it has been passed on from generation to generation and that's how I learned that the door of peace was true.
Teraes Clemmons, Age 9

Once upon a time there was a boy named Josh. He wanted to play football. He saw a wolf playing football. He asked to play. The wolf said, "Sure, do you have any pads?" "No," Josh said, "I want to play peacefully. "Okay," said the wolf.
Austin Hite, Age 9

One warm, peaceful day, my friend Matt and I were on our way to the park to play some baseball. We were riding our bikes when all of the sudden, Blake the bully came out of the bushes. He was going to hurt us with his new shiny brass knuckles. His fist was zooming towards my face like a fireball. I asked him to stop. Right in the nick of time, his fist suddenly stopped. Then I asked him if he would like to be our friend and be a peaceful person like Matt and me. He said he would love to. So we went to the park being peaceful people.
Derek Haffner, Age 10

This is the story of how the snow bear made peace. First the snow bear told the people to make peace. So they did make peace with each other. They became friends.

Next, they met someone else who wasn't making peace. So he said to stop fighting and make peace. They did and they made friends.

Third, he saw people killing and fighting. He said to stop killing and fighting and make peace. So they did make peace and became friends.
Shannon Larkins, Age 9

Thoughts on Peace

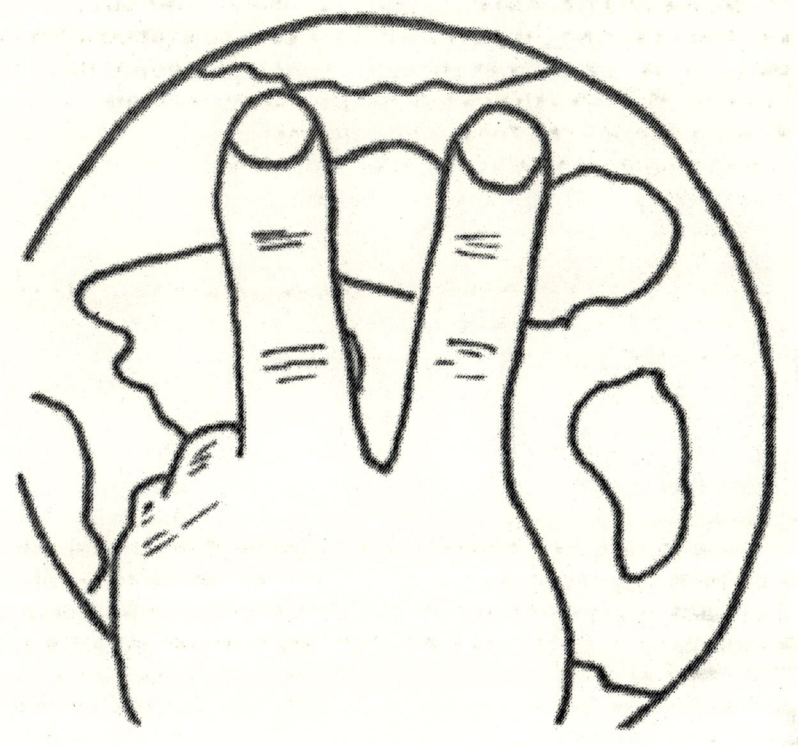

*Artwork by
Brittany Scott, Age 10*

Peace is important because it helps us get through every day. It helps us live healthy lives. It helps make us realize that every day we are lucky to be alive.

Peace shows us that war is wrong. If we were in a war right now this very second, we might not be alive. All this fighting going on needs to stop this very second. Stop fighting like three-year-olds, sit down, talk, listen, and compromise.

Work for peace! Let peace begin with you, then your family and friends, your class, your school, your county, your state, your country, and then the world. What a great place to live, in a peaceful place!

Nicole Campbell, Age 11

Peace is the second most important chemical element. Hydrogen is the first. Hydrogen might keep us alive, but peace keeps the life going in good harmony. The mathematical formula for peace is p=pl x s (peace equals people times serenity). Peace on the chemical chart is not in a metal or non-metal area. It is actually in the people-gathering area of the chart.

Peace is also known as a cell in the human body. This cell is found in the brain and the heart. But this cell does not work with other cells and tissues to perform tasks. This cell is independent. Outside of the human body, the peace cell tries to work with all other people on earth.

The peace cell, unlike other cells, does not split to be able to help more. This cell has enough power on its own. In this cell, thick, short lines (known as chromosomes in other cells) are called compassion. Compassion exists to help all people come together to make peace. Tiny orange boxes are the love and caring. These are next after compassion to make the people grouped together work strongly towards their goal of peace. Thin lines overpowering the cell are known as belief. Belief is what makes the people try to make peace by believing in themselves and others. This is how the peace cell works.

This partly concludes the connection between science and peace. But remember, peace should be all through the earth. Peace also has to begin with one person to spread it. Let it begin with you.

Josh Nelson, Age 11

Let peace begin with the world, with our nations, countries, and states.   Let peace begin with faces, Asian, African, Chinese, European, and other kinds of people.   Let peace begin in families, homes, hospitals, businesses, and churches. Most of all, let peace begin with me.

Megan Bright, Age 11

Let peace begin with my home, my family, and friends, and neighbors.

Let peace begin with the homeless and children who lost their parents.

Let peace begin with robbers and murderers and kidnappers and people who live on the streets and don't have a home.

Let peace begin with the children who are in the hospital for a long time and have nothing to heal them.

Let peace begin with the parents who have had their child kidnapped, drowned, or killed in an accident so suddenly.

And Lord, let peace begin with me.

Ashley Jenise Smith, Age 11

There was a young lady named Sharry. She had a special garden with ripe fruit. They all had the love she made them with. The world was facing another war. More than three continents were in a depression. This whole war was about money and claiming territory.

Sharry had so much fruit, she didn't know what to do. It was late. She went to sleep. Sharry had a dream about her fruit and the war. In her dream, she gave fruit to all those who wanted to fight. They ate the fruit and they started to shine. None of them wanted to fight. They came up with a plan to give the countries suffering from depression some money to get back on their feet. Sharry woke up.

The war had started. She got all of the fruit and took them to the war zone. Sharry did what she did in her dream, and it all turned out like her dream.

Stephen Cole, Age 11

One day Leslie was at her friend's house, and they were playing checkers. They got tired of playing that when Leslie's friend Carla heard her Mom calling her in for dinner. She asked Leslie if she wanted to stay for dinner. Leslie said she couldn't stay. Today was her day to wash dishes. So they said they would meet the next day to ride bikes. But the next day Leslie said she couldn't ride bikes until later because her mom needed her help, so Carla got on her bike and left by herself. Leslie went back home, and her mom said she didn't need her help anymore, so she left and went back to find Carla. On the way she saw Carla on the sidewalk crying because she was hurt, so she got Carla's bike and helped her home.
Cheree Lester, Age 12

One day at daycare my friend, Caitlin, and I went outside. We were talking with a lot of people and playing. We started playing hide and go seek. We got into a little argument when we started playing. I told everybody just to be quiet and drop it. So we started to play for like 30 minutes; then we got tired. The boys finally decided what we were going to play. It was football. The girls won 14 to 7. The boys got really mad so we started arguing again. But this time it didn't stop, so I walked away. That's what I learned from my guidance teacher: just walk away. Then they said they were sorry.

Then we played freeze tag. We didn't get into an argument then, but we did stop playing after 15 minutes. A few minutes later, the boys started bugging Caitlin and me, so we told them to go away and leave us alone. We went to play by ourselves on the swing set, then the monkey bars. Here come the boys. We were on the monkey bars, and we were on the edge. Then all the sudden it fell over, so we were under the bar of the monkey bars. I was lucky enough to push the 75-lb. monkey bars off my neck before it fell, but my best friend Caitlin got her fingers mashed. I learned how to be strong in dangerous times.

The next day we found out that the boys had picked it up and made it fall. So that's my story about being strong and being very calm in dangerous times. Always believe in yourself through the tough times and dangerous times. I gained peace by not starting a fight.
Rebecca Pryor, Age 11

Everyone has the opportunity to have peace in their lives. Sometimes it may be hard to achieve. In order for the world to be a better place, everyone must find peace within themselves. The question is, "Why would anyone not want peace in their life?" If we all had peace, there would be no wars or crimes.
Patrick Mabrey, Age 12

War. What does that word mean to you? I don't know what your opinion about it is; but to me, war means violence and killing. These are two words that people think of when they are mad at each other.

One of my friend's dads died in a war. That is the number one reason why I hate war. I also dislike wars because they start by one little comment made by one person in one country about something that is happening in another country. Then another person makes a comment about that comment that the person from the other country made, and then an argument starts.

After a while, the president says, "Yes. We need a good war to set things right with that country." So people start gathering weapons up to go to war and start a "surprise attack." Once the war starts, there is violence and a lot of killing. Once the war ends, only one army has won. The other either surrendered or they have all died out. Those are the main reasons why I don't like wars.
Terry D. King, Age 12

When you're having the worst day of your life, people care. When a loved one has passed away, people care. When you're hurt deep down inside, people care. There are many people on Earth that care. There are also many people who are cruel. People who are cruel need just as much love as people who are as nice as you or I. Just remember, when you are down in the dumps, there are people who care.
James Lynch, Age 12

Once there was a boy. He was new in his neighborhood and he wanted to make friends. But he couldn't do that until school started the next day. Nobody wanted to introduce himself or herself to him, so after school he went home. His mom said, "Did you have a good day?" The boy said, "No, I did not make any friends." Then the next day he met one friend. Then they played together the whole day and became neighbors. The next day he met more friends.
Parker Dee Duncan, Age 8

My story is about a man who would not give up on getting black people to be just as equal as white people. When I say "would not give up," I mean he led the bus boycott and was stabbed in the back for trying to treat people of color like white people.

This man is Martin Luther King, Jr. He was born in 1929. King was a Baptist minister, and he graduated from Morehouse College in 1948 when he was 19. On December 1, 1955, he led a march to Washington and gave his "I Have a Dream" speech. In 1964 he received the Nobel Peace Prize. Then on April 4, 1968, Dr. Martin Luther King, Jr., was assassinated in a Memphis hotel.
Justin Hollis, Age 12

One night I had a very, very strange dream. I was flying in the air in my bed in the middle of a war. I stopped at a polluted lake. Suddenly I realized what I could do after I got out of this dream. That evening, I called Taylor and some of my other friends and we went to that lake and cleaned it up. We stopped a war, stopped pollution, and everyone thought we were cool. That night, Taylor had a very, very strange dream that he was in a war. Taylor was very scared; he found a cave to hide in. He thought about what he could do. He had an idea to make peace by stopping the war. Taylor got both colonels together to talk it out. After six hours, they finally made up their minds to stop the war and make peace. Taylor had one problem – how to get out of this dream. I just slapped him and he woke up.
Jay Frye, Age 9

People have been littering our environment. But some people have been cleaning it, which is good for our environment. Try picking litter up for our environment. Please clean it up! Here is what you need to do to make our environment peaceful: clean it up, plant trees, and make clean waters for fish.
Mikey Roop, Age 8

There are moments in life when you want to pick them from your dreams and hug them. Dream what you want to dream, go where you want to go, be what you want to be because you only have one life, one chance to tell yourself, "I am a good person," and "I try my best to become that person."

May you have enough happiness to make you sweet, enough trials to keep strong, enough sorrow to keep you human, and enough hope to make you happy.

Always put yourself in other people's shoes. If you feel it hurts you, then it surely hurts them, too. The happiest people don't necessarily have the best of everything; they just make the best of everything that comes their way.

Happiness lies for those who cry, those who hurt, those who have searched, and those who have tried. Love begins with a smile, grows with a kiss, and ends with a tear. The brightest future will always be based on a forgotten past.

You can't go on well in life until you let go of your past failures and heartaches. When you were born, you were crying and everyone around you was smiling.

Live your life so when you die, you will be smiling and everyone around you will be crying.
Artie Scarazzo, Age 12

Once there were two girls. A new girl came to school one day. She didn't know anyone and was very lonely and homesick. The lonely girl was swinging on the swing at recess, and the two girls waved at her. With a happy smile on her face, she asked them to play with her. The three girls became friends. The next day, the new girl asked them if she could play with them again. When they played together, they were all happy. So they played together every day, and they became great friends. Look what a wave and a smile can do.
Grace Phillips, Age 8

There was a boy. His name was Rick. Robbers killed his parents. He ran away from the orphanage. Then he decided to stop violence. He knew he couldn't do it alone, but he tried.

First, he got a job. Five years later he turned twenty and once again lived alone. First he stopped poaching. Then he stopped robberies. After three years, he put a stop to everything but wars. It took him ten years to stop the wars, but when he did, he got a surprise. His parents were still alive. They said they were in a play and had to fake death. He lives with them now.

Stevie Belew, Age 10

As the snowflakes dance all around, I lay and make an angel on the ground. On the way home, I look to see a homeless person all alone. I wonder if he did something bad, or if he planned something, and it didn't go as he thought it would. If you think something is always going to go as you plan, think again. If you know something you did or you are about to do is wrong, before you do it, think. If you've already done it, ask for forgiveness. Our precious Lord always forgives. Why can't there be love like the man above. Is God so fed up with all our sins and our not asking for forgiveness that He's just trying to teach us a lesson? Or is it the Devil trying to ruin a beautiful blessing?

Life is complicated. I don't understand. I wish someone would take my hand and guide me through. I can help someone too. I guess what I'm trying to say is that, as long as we ask for forgiveness, everything will work out fine.

One day I'll walk the line. One day I'll ask how life works. But until then, I'll try to understand and ask for forgiveness. I think you should too.

Brittanie Howell, Age 12

How can we stop a crime? There are so many things in mind. Open your eyes and see what a shame it is to commit a crime. Why can't there be peace on Earth? That's the way God wants it to be. So, if you see a friend committing a crime, read this poem to them, and I'm sure it will change their mind.

Whitney Strong, Age 11

On Christmas Eve, I had forgotten to get my mom her Christmas present. So I went to Wal-Mart before it closed for the night. When I got in, I saw all the people, and I got really mad. I rushed through the people and took a short cut through the toy department. I ran into a little kid, and his grandma said that he didn't have enough money to get the doll he was holding. She told him to stay right there, and she would be right back.

He started to cry when she walked away. I asked him what the matter was, and he told me. He said that his mom was going to see his sister, and he wanted her to give this doll to her because she wasn't here to receive it for her birthday. So I gave him some extra money to help him get the doll. When I gave him the money, he looked at me and smiled and said thank you. Three weeks later I read in the paper that a mother had died, and I thought to myself, "Is this the boy's mother he was talking about?" So I went to the funeral, and sure enough, I saw the boy. When I went up to the casket, there was the doll he had held in his hand that day.
Talia Mowry, Age 12

There should be love and peace everywhere so there would not be any robberies or any people being killed. People would live with the person they love and live with their families, and live in peace and happiness.
Sean Guajuardo, Age 11

One day my friends and I were outside playing in the yard. A new kid on the block came over to play with us, and he turned out to be a bully. We were playing on our scooters, and he took my scooter and rode off with it down the street. When I tried to get my scooter back, he would not give it back and was laughing as he rode farther down the street. He finally came back to my house with my scooter, and I was able to get it back. I told him he should not take another kid's toys without asking. I told him he was a bully and that he should go home. I told him to come back when he could be more of a friend and play better with others. The next week the boy came back over to my house and apologized to me and we made peace. We played together all day and had a great time on our scooters.
Travis Hamer, Age 9

Our characters are a girl named Lisa; she is caring. There is also a girl named Katelyn who doesn't know anything about church.

It was Sunday. Lisa's family was going to church. Lisa asked Katelyn to go with her. Katelyn said, "What is church?" "It's a place where you worship God," Lisa said. "Who is God?" Katelyn asked. "A very good man that lives in heaven," Lisa said. "I don't like church. It's stupid. I want to stay home and play," Katelyn said. Lisa asked another girl named Hannah. Hannah said yes. So they went to church. She started going every Sunday. But Katelyn never went. God came into Hannah's heart but not Katelyn's. When they had all grown up, Lisa and Hannah wanted to talk to Katelyn. They talked to her. She started to go to church every Sunday until she died.
Hannah Reeder, Age 8

One day, a long time ago, we had a war. And our world was destroyed. People did not have any homes because of that. People had to chop down trees and kill animals to get food. Mothers' babies were killed too. You can help the earth by growing trees and stop killing animals. If you don't want to live outside, then save the earth. I'm going to save the earth by growing trees, not killing animals, not killing people, not throwing trash outside, and being gentle to people.
Brooke Schultz, Age 9

Gangs are bad, dangerous, and stupid.
First, gangs are bad. It is not good to be in a gang. You can waste your life.
Second, gangs are dangerous. You could get shot and die or go to jail.
Third, gangs are stupid. It is stupid to be in a gang. You have to do stuff to get in, like killing someone. Or ten guys get on each side of you with paddles and you have to walk through them. So if you go in a gang, you are stupid.
Matt Campbell, Age 12

Why do people steal and kill? Why do we have to lock our doors and windows? Why do people have to be so mean? Why do you think they are doing this? Is it in anger or sadness? Let's pray it's not for fun.

People need to stop and think about the people they have hurt. I wish that one day I could go to bed and not have to worry about someone coming in and killing me. I don't want to bring kids into this bad place. I don't want to worry about being raped or kidnapped. That is what I don't want the world to be like.

Lauren Hughes, Age 11

When I grow up, I wonder if people will be afraid to cry or to die. Will I be able to see a rainbow in a small field sky? Will there be any trees alive? If not, how will the planet survive? Will there be an internet at www? A lifetime air supply?

When I grow up and I get bored, can my son and I build a canoe? That water used to be so blue. Will it be so polluted it will give people the flu?

When I grow up, will doors be made of hammers or nails? Will schools be built next door to jails? Will the truth be illegal to sell?

When I grow up, will anybody be on the news for anything besides killing? Will those drug dealers still be standing there in front of my building? Will they ever learn or stay afraid of the feeling?

When I grow up, will students be going home in a bullet-proof bus? What if children had no one to trust? That would hurt me so much and I want to be happy when I grow up...

Chelsea Browning, Age 12

I think that the world is a gift like life is, and you should never take one day of it for granted! I think that you should always treat others the way you like to be treated! So, let peace begin with you and me!

Sarah Sturges, Age 11

I could keep the bad guys or girls away from other houses by calling the police. I could graduate from college and be a police girl. I would be kind and nice to elderly people. I would also not hurt anyone unless I had to defend myself. If my buddy tried to start a fight, I would just count to five and walk away. I would be kind and let someone in front of me if we were in line.
Chelsea Mabry, Age 10

One night I was at work with my mom at Middle Tennessee Mental Health Institute. Two twin 6-year-old girls walked in with their mother. She admitted them and said that they were disrespecting her, but they weren't. The mother had cut one of the girl's hair off to look like a boy's haircut because she wanted a boy, not a girl. The girl had beautiful blonde hair and blue eyes. The little girl was even dressed like a little boy, too.

I believe I could prevent this in the world by reminding people to watch out for abused children. If you are aware of someone being abused, please encourage them to do their best in life or be the best they can be in life. Also talk to the person who is abusing them and encourage them to stop, because they can do better in life than just sit around waiting to abuse someone or something.
Leigh Ann Allison, Age 11

Don't use guns and knives for violence. Be nice to anybody you meet. Do not take drugs. Put a gate at the entrance of a community. Don't fight with others. Stand up for others. Tell them not to fight.
Devon Mason, Age 9

Have you been scared to send your child to school? You had an argument that morning, and you are worried that you won't ever see your kid again? Well, it's happened to some people. I feel sorry for the people it happened to. I would rather it had happened to me than for a kid under five years old ever to be hurt because they never experienced school or friends.
James Cody Lemaster, Age 12

Once upon a time, a boy and his two friends made a plan to stop fighting, help others, and stop violence in their neighborhood.
Preston Summers, Age 8

Once upon a time, two kids named Josh and Taylor got tired of trash on the road. To make a difference in the world, they had to clean the world by themselves. They did it together. They did the first job on Friday, and they did it together. It was never messy again. They got trophies for teamwork, respect, and citizenship.
Robbe Phillips, Age 11

Hi. My name is Larry, and today is a boring day at school. We had to watch an old 60s film. It's about a kid with five bullies. They give him a hard time. So, it's going to be very boring.

I was watching the movie and I fell asleep. When I woke up, I wondered where I was. Wow! I was in the old 60s movie. I heard a kid screaming and saw the kid from the movie running from the bullies. "Stop!" I said, but they could not hear me. "Am I a ghost?" I asked the kid. "Do you want someone to help you stop them?"

"Sure," he said.

"O.K., when they come back, let me handle it."

When the bullies came back, I told them to just move on and not hurt the kid. They said, "O.K. Maybe you're right."

The kid thanked me and I said, "You're welcome."
Hunter Keller, Age 11

I would help people who don't have food or money. I would teach kids to say no to drugs and also teach my little brother and sister to say no to drugs. If they pass it to their friends, and if everybody passes it, then no one would sell drugs. I would make up peace because it would help people who do drugs to stop. If we tell people to stop, I would say nicely to them, it would be good for you if you could stop the drug thing.
Shelby Paris, Age 8

87

Peace Is...

Artwork by
Ashley Hall, Age 10

Peace is
No violence,
Caring for each other,
Being respectful,
Helping each other,
Peaceful world,
Quiet,
Making new friends,
Being nice,
Believing in good not evil, and
Working together.
That's what peace is to me.
Rachel Pardue, Age 10

Let peace begin with me.
Let peace begin with you.
But most of all, let peace begin with God.
Natalie Graves, Age 10

Peace
Quiet, lovely
Swaying, leaped, sleep
Happy, relaxed comfortable, calm
Freedom
Chelsea Atnip, Age 9

Peace
Amity, friendship
Quiet, peaceful, serenity
Calm, undisturbed, composed, quiet
Tranquility
Nicole Paschall, Age 9

Peace
Joy, nice
Sleep, smile, laugh,
Happy, jolly, wonderful, excellent
Quiet
Amanda Anderson, Age 10

Harmony, quiet
Helping, giving, praying
Happy, joyful, hopeful, love
Freedom
Gabrielle Ford, Age 10

Quiet, calm
Nice, joyful, happy
Hopeful, lovely, cordial, great
Freedom
Brandon Hibner, Age 10

Partnership
Equal
Acceptable
Comfort
Effort

Agreement,
Ability, able,
Acclaim, calm, quite,
Relaxing, peaceful, peaceable, polite,
Shy
Trisha Ramsey, Age 9

People
Can get along
With everybody if they want
So we *can* make a better world.
Amen.
Dallas Dwenger, Age 11

Peace is
Quiet,
Nice,
Not mean,
Caring,
Responsible,
Respectful,
Fair,
Trustworthy
That's what peace is.
Chase Chandler, Age 10

Love
Happiness
Health
Friendship
No guns
Longer lives
No violence
And
A nice place!
That is what peace means to me!
Emily Jean Anderson, Age 9

W.A. Wright Elementary School

No wars
Calmness
Quietness
Love
No arguing
Joy
Harmony
Kindness
Goodness
Peaceable place
Gentleness
That's what peace is to me
Kayla Connelly, Age 10

Peace is
No shooting
No killing
No stealing
No mean faces
No fighting
A lot of peace
Kindness
Peace is fun
Peace is the right way
That's what peace is.
Steven Fort, Age 11

In a world full of war and hate, think of our beautiful skies of blue.

In a world that has both feast and famine, think of our oceans and the crashing waves.

When we are feeling too proud, let us stand at the mountaintop and feel the wind.

Think of what would happen if it were all gone.

Remember that peace begins with me.
Laura Wauford, Age 10

Quiet
No fighting
No taking drugs
No killing others
Respect others
Being friendly and nice
Sharing
Smiling at people
Caring
Being trustworthy
Rebecca Peterson, Age 9

Peace is
Alone
Being different
Reading
Silence
Sleeping
Drawing
No Fighting
Friends
Love
That's Peace to me
Tommy Lynch, Age 9

Peace
Peaceful
Enjoy
A day without war
Calm
Erasing conflict
Taryn King, Age 10

Nice
Courteous
Obedient, Helpful
Kyle Vandierendonck, Age 10

W.A. Wright Elementary School

Peace
Bright, joyful
Happy, glad, hopeful
Helping, caring, nice
Freedom
Selina Smith, Age 9

Violence doesn't solve anything
In our hearts
Only loving not hating counts
Leave the hating behind you
Everything counts in this world
No violence
Care for all people
Everyone is a loving person
Jessica Guajardo, Age 10

My Hope for Peace is
That everyone goes to church.
No more violence.
No more drugs.
For everyone to share.
To have a home.
To have food.
To have money.
Travis Spicer, Age 10

I like
Peace in the world
People need to not fight
I hope people get along with kids
Good bye
Mikey Weaver, Age 10

Peace
Peaceful, harmony
Caring, helping, loving
MLK, butterfly, Civil War, World War II
Fighting, killing, bleeding
Violence, firearms
War
Douglas Garrison, Age 9

Peace is here if you look and see.
Peace is somewhere tonight.
Peace is looking at thee.

(Chorus)
Peace, peace, peace, peace is in ye.
Peace in your heart
Peace, peace, peace, peace is in ye.
Peace in your heart
Peace, peace, peace, peace is in ye.
Peace in your heart

Peace is all around ye.
Peace is in the air tonight.
Peace is here ye! *(x2)*

(Repeat chorus)
Tyler Bell, Age 9

Let there be peace in me. Let there be peace. Let there be peace in me. Let there be peace. Peace in the world and peace in me. Peace is all over you. You just have to see. Peace is something quiet and harmony. You have to look around and you will see peace. Let there be peace in me. Let there be peace. Let there be peace in me. Let there be peace. Peace in the world. People have peace in schools, churches, and in me.
Lauren Self, Age 10

Peace
Nice, quiet
Loving, pleasing, loved
Pleased, pleasing, fighting, bad
Robbing, stealing, cursing
Poison, evil
Devil
Kasey Coble, Age 9

Peace is:
No violence,
Being respectful,
Caring for others,
Quiet,
Being friendly,
No drugs,
Not interrupting others,
That's what peace is to me.
A.J. Wright, Age 10

Peace is:
Getting along,
Being Nice,
Friendship,
Loving,
Caring,
Respect,
That's what peace means to me.
Allison Cantrell, Age 10

Let us have peace.
A life of joy and happiness.
No wars. No terror. No grief.
We can all live together as a family.
Only love can be found.
No hatred to be seen.
Let us have peace.
Jessie Blankenship, Age 10

I look out my window and what do I see?
I see homeless
I see violence

I wish it all would stop
I know I'm just a child, but I can do stuff too

(Chorus)
Let there be peace on earth
Oh, let there be peace
Let there be peace on earth
Oh, let there be peace

I walk out my door and what do I see?
I see guns
I see drugs
If only we could agree
And do stuff to help

(Repeat Chorus)

I walk into town and what do I see?
I see smoking
I see killing
Oh, I see alcohol and littering
Let's just work together and see what we can do

(Repeat Chorus)
Ashley Mitchell, Age 10

Let the world
Open
Its eyes
And see
The light
And have
Peace
On
Earth
Alex Engel, Age 11

Today wars break out
People dying every second
What if we just changed?
Brent Fite, Age 11

A Caring fellow.
Helping those that are needed
Caring for people.
Bijan Stegall, Age 10

We need peace
On our earth
For our children

If we fight
We'll sometimes lose
And maybe lose
Our children

Think about the children
Think for some children
Talk to children about wars
Tell them the horrors
They'll listen
They won't try to get wars started
They'll try to stop them
Talk to your children!
Ronica Haynes, Age 11

Love is deep
So is peace.
Let it be
In you and me.
Chet Allen, Age 11

Religion
Injustice
Good
Holy
Time
Justin Caires, Age 12

I would think the world would be a better place if no one did drugs, drank alcohol, or broke laws. People don't understand how to take care of the world. I'm against violence and doing drugs. This is how I think. So let peace begin with me.
Kelsey Elliot, Age 11

Help people around the world
Help children without family, food, and shelter
Help them have a home with a family and food to eat
Help people without groceries
Help people who need someone to talk to
Help neighbors with yard work
Find homes for lost animals
Help people understand why things are going to happen
Have fun and smile at the bad and the good
Help a friend when they are down
Help them understand they are not the only one
Help stop crime and violence
Help everyone around you that you possibly can and the world will end up having a better image.
Angela Bogle, Age 12

W.A. Wright Elementary School

Let there be peace,
And let it begin with me.

Let peace begin with me,
Let people be free.

Let peace begin with me,
Let people be!
Brett Schultz, Age 11

Fruit is good and so are you
We need you all the time
If you use peace
You solve problems
Here are some rules to solve them:
Identify the problem
Focus on the problem
Attack the problem
Peace contains
Citizenship
Respect
Trustworthiness
Fairness
Responsibility
and
Caring
Kari Taylor, Age 11
Stefani Langston, Age 11

Acknowledgements

W.A Wright would like to give its
sincere appreciation to
John Deal Company, Inc.
JDC, Inc.
and
SPI, Inc.
for their sponsorship of
Let Peace Begin With Me
and for their
continuing support of education.

John Deal Company, Inc.

JDC, Inc.

SPI, Inc.